BLAST TO THE PAST

#2

Bell's Breakthrough

By Stacia Deutsch
and Rhody Cohon
Illustrated by David Wenzel

Aladdin Paperbacks
New York London Toronto Sydney

**To those who showed me the writer's path:
the women of Ohio Valley, especially Jan Scarbrough
and Toni Blake. Kathy Flake, writer, reader,
and promoter extraordinaire. And Hilary Sares,
who gave me my first break. And to my husband who
supported me throughout my journey.
Thank you.
—Stacia Deutsch**

**Thanks to my family for their love and support.
—Rhody Cohon**

ALADDIN PAPERBACKS
An imprint of Simon & Schuster Children's Publishing Division
1230 Avenue of the Americas, New York, NY 10020
Text copyright © 2005 by Stacia Deutsch and Rhody Cohon
Illustrations copyright © 2005 by David Wenzel
All rights reserved, including the right of reproduction
in whole or in part in any form.
ALADDIN PAPERBACKS and colophon are trademarks of
Simon & Schuster, Inc.
Designed by Lisa Vega
The text of this book was set in Minion.
Manufactured in the United States of America
First Aladdin Paperbacks edition October 2005
2 4 6 8 10 9 7 5 3 1
The Library of Congress Control Number 2004118394
ISBN-13: 978-0-689-87026-2
ISBN-10: 0-689-87026-4

Contents

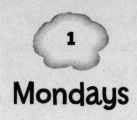

Mondays

"Hello, Abigail," Mr. Caruthers said when I opened the classroom door.

I blinked twice.

"Mr. Caruthers?" I was surprised to see my teacher sitting at his desk. Our teacher was always late to class on Mondays. And he usually sat on his desk, never behind it.

I popped my head back into the hallway. The sign on the door read, THIRD GRADE. SOCIAL STUDIES. ROOM 305.

There was no mistake. I was definitely in the right place.

Something weird was going on.

"Good morning, Zack and Jacob," Mr. Caruthers

greeted the twins as they entered behind me.

"Huh?" Zack said, staring blankly at our teacher. He was confused too.

We hurried to our table. Zack, Jacob, and I sit with a new kid named Roberto Rodriguez. Maybe he knew what was up.

"Hey, Bo," Jacob whispered. "What's Mr. C doing here?" Our teacher was so cool, we always called him Mr. C.

Bo answered in a voice so soft, I could barely hear him. "I was the first one to class. When I saw him at his desk, I thought I was in the wrong room. I almost left." Bo was so quiet and shy, it wasn't hard to imagine him leaving the classroom and running away. He doesn't like talking to grown-ups. I was actually kind of surprised he stayed. He must really like Social Studies. Or Mr. C.

"I did the same thing," I said. I pulled out my chair and sat down.

It was totally strange.

Every Monday, Mr. Caruthers was five minutes late to class.

Every Monday, his clothes were wrinkled and messy.

Every Monday, his glasses sat way down on his nose. And his hair stuck up, way up to the sky.

But today, he was on time. His suit was neat. His tie was tied. His glasses were where they were supposed to be. Even his hair was combed.

And he was *sitting* in his chair!

"Is it really Monday?" I asked Zack.

"I think so," Zack answered. "Do you think this has something to do with T.T.?"

"T.T?" I questioned. "What's T.T.?"

Zack leaned over and put his hand around my ear. "Time travel," he whispered.

I didn't say anything. I just winked one eye and nodded.

Bo, Jacob, Zack, and I knew the secret reason why Mr. C was messy and late on Mondays.

Mr. C was an inventor. In his private, hidden laboratory under the school, Mr. C had created a time-travel computer. It looked like a handheld video game, but when he put a special cartridge in the back, a smoky, green, glowing time-travel hole opened in the floor.

He was always messy because when he made the cartridge there was a wicked explosion. The time-travel cartridge didn't work without the explosion.

We thought the reason he was always late to class was because he was time traveling, but we were wrong. Mr. C told us he was always late because he was working on another, brand-new, hush-hush invention. He barely slept, and never had time to change clothes or shower. On Monday mornings he'd rush to class after the bell had already rung.

We knew his secrets because Jacob, Zack, Bo, and I were Mr. C's helpers.

Mr. C wanted more time to focus on his new invention, so he asked us to time-travel for him. He explained to us that American history was in danger. He showed us a little black book full of names. For some mysterious reason, all the famous Americans on Mr. C's list were quitting. They weren't inventing, or speaking out, or fighting for what was right. They were giving up on their dreams!

Our mission was to save history from changing forever!

We time-traveled on Mondays during the after-school club time.

It was weird. We would leave on a Monday, but it wasn't always a Monday when we arrived in the past. We would leave at three o'clock, but it wasn't always three o'clock when we got to the past. And yet, the clock ticks at the same speed in the past as it does in our time. Time travel is crazy like that!

So far, we'd been very successful in our adventures. We'd managed to keep history on track—no small thing, since the computer only gives us two hours to get the job done.

We didn't know what would happen if we went over the two-hour limit. And we didn't want to know. The time-travel computer might have a freak-out. And if we weren't home by the end of club time, so would our parents. That is why we had to hustle and be careful about how much time we spent in the past.

Every Monday, we crossed our fingers and hoped

that Mr. Caruthers would send us on another adventure. But lately, instead of T.T., Mr. C kept sending us to the library! The past two Monday afternoons, we'd been sitting around, reading boring books about Alexander Graham Bell.

Brrring.

The bell rang. It was time for class to start.

Mr. Caruthers stood up from his chair. He cleared his throat and asked, "What if Alexander Graham Bell had quit and never invented the telephone?" Our whole class loved Mr. C's "what if?" questions. He asked them every Monday.

Could today's "what if?" question be a clue? Could it be our day to go on a T.T. adventure? Mr. C had made us read about Alexander Graham Bell in the library. Now, he was asking about Alexander Graham Bell in class. I didn't want to get too excited, just in case I was wrong.

I looked over at the boys. I wanted to ask them if they thought the Alexander Graham Bell question might be a sign. I stared at Jacob. He didn't look at me. Then I stared at Bo. He wasn't looking at me either. So I tried staring at the side of Zack's head until my eyes hurt.

It was useless.

Bo, Jacob, and Zack each had his hand raised. They weren't thinking about T.T. anymore. They were thinking about the question.

I decided to forget about T.T. for a little while too. I raised my hand because I knew what my life would be like if Alexander Graham Bell had never invented the telephone.

I wanted to tell Mr. C how horrible it would be if there were no telephones. The world would feel so big and disconnected.

I'd have to walk to my friends' houses and wait for them to get home. I'd have to write letters to my relatives who lived far away. And wait for them to write back. I'd have to wait to see my parents just so I could ask them a question.

Without telephones, my whole life would be spent waiting around. I'm definitely not good at

waiting. In fact, I am probably the most impatient person in the whole entire universe.

I wanted to tell Mr. C what I thought, so I raised my hand higher and waved it in the air. I bounced in my seat, trying to get Mr. C's attention. I wiggled so much, I nearly fell off my chair.

Mr. C called on Gitma. She said that Alexander Graham Bell's invention of the telephone had made a whole bunch of other things possible, like voice mail, call-waiting, cell phones, text messaging, the Internet, and e-mail.

Mr. C called on Rishad. He said that without the phone, there'd be no fax machines. Rishad had never sent a fax. But his dad sent them every day at work.

Mr. C had called on every kid in the room. Except me.

When class was over, I felt like I'd been kicked in the stomach. Mr. C *always* called on me! I didn't understand what had happened.

I'm a good student. I have good ideas. I was angry with Mr. Caruthers for ignoring me. So I marched up to Mr. C to ask him why he hadn't called on me. "What's going on?" I asked boldly. "You never called—"

Mr. C put up one hand and stopped me. "Abigail," he said in a low, clipped voice, "I'll see you after school, right?"

"But—," I began again.

"Abigail," Mr. C repeated. "Three o'clock in the library."

I sighed. I didn't feel like wasting another stupid Monday in the library, reading about Alexander Graham Bell. But if I ever wanted to time-travel again, I didn't have a choice. "Yes, Mr. Caruthers," I mumbled. "I'll be there."

Then, to make a strange Monday even stranger, Mr. Caruthers winked.

2

T.T.

Jacob was waiting for me by the door to the library.

"What was the deal with Mr. C today?" Jacob asked in a whispered voice. We walked past the librarian's desk and headed to our regular meeting place.

"I have no idea," I answered. I counted the weirdnesses on my fingers: "He was dressed neatly. He was on time. He sat at his desk. He didn't call on me. And he winked at me when I was leaving." I wiggled all five fingers. "Yep, it was a very weird morning."

Jacob started to say something back, but we saw Bo waving at us. We stopped talking and walked faster instead.

Bo was sitting on a corner couch. There was a big

stack of books on the table next to him. Bo loved to read. He was taking this extra assignment very seriously.

Bo picked up a book off the table. It was a copy of Mr. C's favorite book: *Famous People in American History.* Bo flipped through the pages and handed the open book to me.

I read the title of the chapter out loud: "'Alexander Graham Bell and His Many Inventions.'" I let out a long breath. It was definitely going to be another dull day in the library.

A minute later, Zack showed up. He put down his backpack and settled onto the couch. But before he leaned back, Zack noticed Jacob's left foot. "Your shoelace is untied," he told his brother.

"I know," Jacob answered. "I like it that way."

"You're going to trip," Zack warned. "You'll break your leg. Or maybe you'll slip and spill something."

"I will not," Jacob countered. "My shoes are always untied. Do you see me falling all over the place?"

"Just tie your shoe!" Zack demanded, but Jacob ignored him. Zack's face turned a little red, as if he was ready to pick a fight. But he must have decided to forget it, because he slumped back onto the couch instead.

I looked down at the book in my hands. There were a lot of pictures on the page. "Look at all these other things Alexander Graham Bell invented," I said, pointing to the pictures. "I thought he just made phones." I gave Bo back the book.

"He was a tinkerer," Bo explained. "Alexander Graham Bell worked on projects for a while until he got tired of them. Then he gave up and went to work on something else."

"What else did he tinker with?" Jacob was curious. Jacob was a tinkerer too. He loved computers and was always taking them apart and rebuilding them. Sometimes he'd use old computer parts to make other cool stuff.

"Alexander Graham Bell invented tons of things," Bo answered. "After the telephone, he worked on air-conditioning, a high-speed boat, a bullet detector, and a way to send information over rays of light. He even tried inventing the airplane."

"I thought the Wright brothers invented the airplane," I questioned.

"They did," Bo said. "But Alexander Graham Bell was also working on an airplane around the same time. He did get his plane to fly, but it was after the Wright brothers had already made history with the first flight."

"Cool," I commented. "Alexander Graham Bell must have been one busy guy."

"Yeah," Bo agreed, then he turned the book toward Jacob. "Look. This is a photo of Bell's drawing for the first telephone. But here it says that Alexander Graham Bell wasn't trying to make a phone. He was working on inventing a multiple telegraph."

"A what?" I asked.

"A multiple telegraph," a deep voice said from behind me. I turned around to find Mr. Caruthers standing over my shoulder. He was holding a small box under his arm. "In eighteen seventy-five, Alexander Graham Bell was working on a way for people to send many telegrams at once," Mr.

Caruthers explained. He put the box down on the couch and took off the lid.

Inside, there was a small metal machine. It had short legs, springs, and a little lever to press.

"I read about telegrams last Monday," Jacob said excitedly.

Mr. Caruthers handed Jacob the telegraph machine.

Jacob pushed the lever down and released it. The telegraph machine made a clicking sound. "In the olden days, if you wanted to send your friend a letter really quickly, you could send a telegram. It was sort of like old-fashioned e-mail."

"I read the same book," Zack said, taking the telegraph machine from his brother. "I even read it before Jacob." He grinned, showing all his teeth.

Zack pressed the lever. He made a few long taps. Then he pressed the lever really quickly, making a *click-clack* sound.

"Short taps are called 'dots,'" Zack said. "Long taps are called 'dashes.' In Morse code, dots and dashes stand for the letters of the alphabet. A person at the post office would type your letter in Morse code and send the code over a wire," he explained. "At a different post office, a person would write down the alphabet letters as they came in. They would decipher the code. And there was your letter!" Zack handed the machine back to Mr. Caruthers.

I was surprised at how much the boys knew about telegraph machines and telegrams. Clearly, I'd been reading the wrong books. I knew a lot about Alexander Graham Bell's life when he was a kid.

Mr. Caruthers put the telegraph machine back in the box and then explained, "Alexander Graham Bell was working on a multiple telegraph when he started to think about sending voices instead of dots and dashes. On March 10, 1876, he invented the telephone."

"Bo told us he changed his mind a lot," I said to Mr. Caruthers. "I guess he changed from inventing telegraphs to inventing telephones."

Mr. Caruthers nodded. It was then that I noticed Mr. Caruthers had changed too. He'd changed clothes.

I looked at Mr. Caruthers more carefully. No, he

hadn't changed clothes. He was wearing the same suit. Only it was messy. Really messy!

I looked at him even more closely. His tie was untied. His glasses were crooked. And his hair—it looked like mine before I brushed it in the morning!

Now I knew it was really Monday! He must have made a brand-new cartridge. That's why he was so messy.

"I need you to go on a time-travel mission," Mr. Caruthers confirmed.

"Yippee!" I cheered. I turned to the boys. They were shouting and making up silly, happy handshakes.

"Shh," Mr. Caruthers said, laughing. "I guess you were tired of reading in the library?"

"You know it!" I quietly cheered.

Suddenly, Mr. C's face got still, and he became serious. "Alexander Graham Bell quit."

My heart began to race. It was time.

We knew what we had to do. We had to convince Alexander Graham Bell to invent the telephone.

"I'm sorry I didn't ask you kids to time-travel the last two weeks, but I wanted you to prepare for today's mission," Mr. C said, and ran a hand over his tangled hair. It flattened for a second, then popped right back up again.

"Yesterday, I got so caught up working on my new invention, I forgot to make the cartridge." He shrugged apologetically. "I just finished it."

Mr. C had told us that whatever he was working on was top secret. I was just about to try to sneak in a question about the new invention when Mr. Caruthers handed Jacob the time-travel computer and a cartridge. The cartridge had a picture of a telephone on it.

When I saw the cartridge, my heart sped up another beat. We had two hours to convince Alexander Graham Bell to finish inventing the telephone.

I decided to ask about the new invention another time. We had to get started! I didn't want to think about my life without telephones. "We're ready," I told Mr. Caruthers.

Jacob slipped the new cartridge into the back of the computer. A glowing green hole opened in the floor next to a tall shelf of books. There was thick smoke floating across the floor.

Bo didn't hesitate. He jumped in first.

"How are we going to find Alexander Graham Bell?" Zack asked before jumping. Zack liked to time-travel, but he worried a lot. "We're going to eighteen seventy-six and we don't know where he is. And we can't call him." Zack was also very funny.

"We'll find him," I assured Zack.

With a big sigh, Zack followed Bo into the hole.

"Hey, Mr. Caruthers," I said, turning back to our teacher. "Why didn't you call on me in class today?"

"I didn't mean to turn a deaf ear," Mr. Caruthers said, as if that would make it all crystal clear.

"What do you mean?" I asked.

"You'll figure it out," Mr. C replied. "It's a clue to help you understand Alexander Graham Bell." Our teacher was certainly one mysterious guy.

"But I don't understand," I said, stepping forward. "What do you mea—"

I never finished my question because I tripped over Jacob's shoelace. As I fell into the hole, I grabbed Jacob's arm and pulled him in with me.

3

Boston, Massachusetts

"Oof," I said as I crash-landed on top of Jacob. I had no idea where we were. We were definitely inside a room, but it was so dark, I couldn't even see my hands. I waved them around a bit to check. Nope. I couldn't see anything.

"Sorry I tripped you," Jacob said from somewhere beneath me.

"I told you to tie your shoe," Zack scolded Jacob. "Abigail could have broken her neck."

"No one got hurt," Jacob told his brother. "I like it untied."

Jacob and I fumbled around a bit, but we finally managed to stand up in the darkness. I felt Jacob move away. I think he had his hands outstretched in front of him, because that's what I always do when it's dark.

"Ouch," Zack said. "Jacob, watch where you're going! You just poked me in the eye." Yep, he definitely had his hands straight out.

"Sorry," Jacob said. I could hear him dragging his hand along the wall looking for a light switch. "Were there lights in eighteen seventy-six?" he asked.

"You aren't going to find a switch," Bo said. "They had gaslights."

"How do you turn on a gaslight?" Jacob asked, but before Bo could reply, there was a big crash. Then a smaller banging sound.

A voice said, "Ouch."

Then Jacob said, "Uh-oh."

I had no idea who'd said "Ouch." It was a female voice. I thought I was the only girl in the room.

I stumbled in the darkness toward what I thought might be a window. It was.

I pulled back the curtains. Sunlight flooded the room.

We were in a bedroom. There was a young woman

lying on the bed. She looked like she was just a few years older than CeCe, my sister. CeCe is sixteen.

Then I saw Jacob. He was lying on the floor. A large bowl with flowers on it was upside down on his head. Jacob must have stumbled in the dark, bumped into the young woman's small table, and fallen near her bed.

"Oh," the young woman said, looking at each of us in turn. Her eyes were wide, and her jaw was hanging open. She was surprised to see us in her room.

"Oops," Zack said. "We're definitely in the wrong place." He went to the door and put his hand on the knob. "We'd better go."

"Do you think the computer messed up?" I asked Jacob.

Jacob took the bowl off his head and put it gently on the floor. Then he looked at the computer. He pressed a few buttons. "It says we're in the right time. It's March 10, 1876."

"But we're not in the right place, so let's get out of here," Zack said, tilting his head toward the door.

"Excuse me," the young woman said from the bed.

"If you are speaking to me, you must look at me. I am deaf. But if you turn toward me, I can read your lips."

Wow! I wanted to stay and talk to her more. I wanted to learn what it was like to read lips. But Zack was right: We didn't have a lot of time. We had to find Alexander Graham Bell. "We have to go," I said, making sure I was looking at her when I spoke.

"Wait!" the woman called. "Please. Stay a few minutes."

Zack shook his head. He pointed to his wrist. He didn't have a watch, but I knew what he meant. We didn't have time to waste.

I held up a finger to Zack and said, "Give me one minute." I sat down on the side of the bed. "Hi, I'm Abigail. These are my friends." I introduced the boys.

"My name is Mabel Hubbard," the girl replied. She was very pretty. And very pale.

"Are you sick?" I asked.

"Yes." She sniffled and pulled a handkerchief out from under her pillow. "I have been in bed more than a week. I feel better, but Father will not let me travel to Aleck's workshop until I am cured."

"I understand," I started to say. "I had a cold once and I missed three days of school—" I stopped suddenly. "Aleck? Who's Aleck?" I asked.

"Alexander Graham Bell," Mabel said, smiling. "The man I am going to marry."

I turned to Zack, who still had his hand on the door. And I winked. "We came to Boston to meet Alexander Graham Bell," I said excitedly. "We have traveled a very long way to see him."

"Are you interested in the multiple telegraph?" Mabel asked, starting to cough. She pointed to a side table, where there was a pitcher of water and a glass. Bo came across the room and poured her some water.

"Thank you," she said, taking a sip of the water. She stopped coughing.

"No. We're not interested in the multiple telegraph," Bo explained. He was so shy, I had to remind him to look up at her when he spoke. "We need to talk to him about the telephone."

"The what?" she asked.

"Telephone," Bo said. "You know, the thing that makes voices go over wires."

"Oh," Mabel said, and laughed. "Aleck is not working on that anymore. Father gave him a lot of money to invent the multiple telegraph. He told Aleck we could not get married until the multiple telegraph was finished."

My jaw dropped open. I couldn't believe her dad was making Alexander Graham Bell quit working on the telephone.

"Father did not force Aleck to quit," she said defensively, as if she knew exactly what I was thinking. "That is just one reason. Aleck is also very tired, and the—what did you call it?"

"Telephone," Zack answered.

"Yes. The telephone." She repeated the word in order to remember it. "The telephone was too much trouble. Aleck is a professor. He teaches deaf children and their teachers all day. Deaf children don't need a machine that carries voices." Mabel sat up in bed. "But everyone could use a multiple telegraph!

And my Aleck is going to make one." She started to cough again.

In our time, no one on earth needed a multiple telegraph. But a lot of people needed telephones. Lots and lots of people used telephones all the time. Every day. There were even special telephones for deaf people.

We needed to find Professor Alexander Graham Bell.

"I guess we should go," Zack said, his hand still on the doorknob. "But I don't think we can convince Professor Bell in time."

"Why not?" Jacob asked his brother.

"Because quitting is easier than trying. Sometimes you don't like doing something, or it doesn't work, or someone tells you that you can't do it, so you just quit."

"You're the expert," Jacob teased his brother. "You're the one who dropped out of Science Club, Theater Club, and the orchestra."

"Yeah. So what? I didn't like any of those things. And I wasn't good at them," Zack said, and stomped his foot on the floor. "All I'm saying is that once I drop out of something, it's almost impossible to convince me to try it again. Like, once I was in orchestra, I wasn't going back to Theater Club. No way. Never. So if Alexander Graham Bell is working on something else now, it's going to be super hard to convince him to go back."

Jacob checked his watch. "Zack, you're talking crazy." He laughed. "Besides, we have plenty of time to convince him. We've got one hour and forty-three minutes left. If you think it's too hard, then we'll convince him without you." Jacob dared his brother to come along.

"I didn't say I wasn't going to help. I'm just saying it's gonna be—" Zack started to say something, then decided to not argue anymore. "Whatever," he mumbled softly. "It's just too bad we don't know where he is."

"Piece of cake," Jacob said, turning his head in the direction of the bed. "Hey, Mabel! Where can we find Professor Bell?"

"I'll have my family's driver take you to him in our

carriage," she offered. "But you must do me a favor."

I was worried that she was going to tell us we could have a ride if we didn't mention the telephone ever again.

But that wasn't it.

Mabel showed us a big, square, flat package that was leaning against the wall near her bed. It was wrapped in brown paper. "Please take this gift to Aleck. It is a portrait I painted of him," Mabel said, smiling widely.

"We'd be happy to deliver it," Bo said. He went and got the package.

"See?" Jacob said, and winked at Zack. "We're already halfway done."

Tricked

I had never been in a carriage pulled by a horse before. I felt like a princess in a parade. It was fun to wave at people on the street as we hurried by.

The carriage stopped in front of a tall, brown brick building.

"Sir," I asked the driver, "do you know where we can find Professor Bell?"

"He lives upstairs," the driver answered. "This is the boardinghouse at 5 Exeter Place."

"A boardinghouse is like an apartment building," Bo told me.

The driver took off his hat and pointed up toward the top of the building. "Professor Bell rents rooms thirteen and fifteen. He uses one for a bedroom and one for a workshop."

"Thanks," Jacob said to the driver as he jumped out of the carriage. He patted the horse on the nose. "And thanks to you, too."

When we were all out of the carriage, Bo handed me Mabel's package for Professor Bell. The four of us hurried up to the building.

Jacob opened the door just as a woman in a yellow coat and matching hat rushed out. She almost crashed into Bo. "Excuse me," she said as she hurried off down the street.

We went inside and immediately smelled something yummy. We followed the scent down a small hallway to a little dining room. There was one man sitting alone at a long table. He was drinking something from a bowl with a tall glass straw.

"More soup!" the man at the long table shouted over his shoulder.

A short lady came out of the kitchen wearing an apron. "Here you are, sir," she said, placing the soup on the table. "Really, you must stop calling me at odd times. Lunch was served hours ago. I am cooking dinner now." She shook her finger at the man. "If you live here, you must obey the rules. Everyone else eats at eight o'clock, noon, and six o'clock."

"I know," the man said, wiping his beard with a napkin. "I get so busy, I lose track of time. But all that is going to change. As of tonight, I shall come to dinner when you call."

"And why is that?" she asked.

"The one thing I wanted to create is too difficult," the man answered with a long sigh. "I quit working on it."

"You have said that before. But you have so many other inventions to keep you busy. I think you will be late again tomorrow." The lady put a bit more soup in his bowl and went back to the kitchen.

"Quit?" Bo whispered.

"He makes inventions, eats at odd hours, and loses track of time!" Jacob cheered. "We found him!" He rushed over to the long table first. "Excuse me, Professor Bell? We are from the future—"

"Future, eh?" the man said. He took his straw out of his soup and set it on the table. The man had a funny accent. I guessed he wasn't born in America.

He laughed. "It is fun to pretend that you are from the future. But I do not have time to play with you. So, shoo. Go on home, now!"

"But, Professor Bell—," Jacob interrupted.

"I am not Professor Bell," the man said. "I am his assistant, Thomas A. Watson." He tipped his hat at us and grinned.

"Yikes!" I said with a shiver. We were bothering the wrong man.

Zack gave Jacob a half-smile. "I warned you this was going to be hard," he gloated.

Mr. Watson explained, "Professor Bell is a smart man, but he is not very good at electrical gadgets. I am a machinist. I help him with the electric part of his inventions." He paused to pick up his straw before continuing.

"Electricity is about making energy," Mr. Watson said. "Energy makes some things move. Energy can make other things get hot, light up, or make noise. I thought—I mean, Professor Bell thought—that electricity could carry sound on a wire. But he was wrong." Mr. Watson shook his head. "We are going to focus our attention on perfecting the multiple telegraph," he finished.

"Can you tell us where to find Professor Bell?" Bo asked in a near whisper. If it might help us find Professor Bell, Bo was willing to talk to an adult (but not very loudly). "We have to tell him to stop working on the multiple telegraph. His most important invention is going to be the telephone."

"The what?" Mr. Watson asked.

"You know—the thing you were just talking about. The thing that makes voices go over wires." Bo held one hand to his mouth and another to his ear, like he was making a phone call.

"How do you know about the electric speech apparatus?" Mr. Watson asked, rubbing the sides of his beard.

I remembered from science class that "apparatus" is a fancy word that means "thing."

Bo opened his mouth to speak, but Mr. Watson

cut him off. "Ah . . . yes, you are from the future." He snickered.

"Well, me laddies"—he looked at me and added—"and me lassie, there is no point in hanging around here. Professor Bell has quit working on electric speech. It doesn't work. He will finish the multiple telegraph, get married, and then go on vacation." He stuck one end of the straw back into his soup. "Now, if you will excuse me, I want to finish my lunch before it grows cold."

He turned away from us and began to slurp. We left the dining room without a clue as to what we'd do next.

We had to talk Alexander Graham Bell out of quitting. Before it was too late.

At the far end of a hallway, Bo noticed a long, tall staircase. The carriage driver had told us that Alexander Graham Bell rented rooms 13 and 15.

Suddenly, Jacob took off running up the stairs two at a time. The boys followed closely on his heels. I was moving a little slower since I was carrying Mabel's painting and it was starting to get heavy.

When I reached the top step, I asked Jacob how much time was left on the computer. It was important to watch our time.

"One hour, twenty-eight minutes," Jacob answered.

None of us knew what would happen if the cartridge ran out of time. And none of us wanted to find out. We had to be careful.

We decided that the fastest way to find Alexander Graham Bell was to split up. Jacob and I went to knock on door 15. No one answered.

Bo and Zack knocked on door 13.

"Hello." A man opened door 13 and stepped into the hall. He was a thin man with a short beard. He was wearing a coat and tie and holding a long piece of wire in his hand.

"Are you Professor Bell?" Zack asked the man.

"No," he answered.

Zack asked, "Isn't this his room?"

"Yes. This is his workshop, but I am Thomas A. Watson," he introduced himself. "I am the machinist who helps Professor Bell."

"Huh?" Bo said. He scratched his chin. He did that

when he was thinking really hard. "We met Mr. Watson downstairs. He has a beard and speaks English with an accent."

The man started laughing. He laughed harder and harder.

"Oh, no!" I exclaimed. "I should have remembered! While you guys were reading about his inventions, I was reading about his childhood. Alexander Graham Bell was born and raised in Scotland!" I smacked myself on the forehead.

"So, that means," Bo said thoughtfully, "that Professor Bell would speak English with an accent."

"Are you saying what I think you're saying?" Jacob asked.

"Yes," Bo said before Jacob finished. "This man *is* Mr. Watson. The real Alexander Graham Bell is downstairs drinking soup with a straw."

I groaned loudly. "We've been tricked!"

5

Alexander Graham Bell

We could still hear Mr. Watson's laughter as we started running back down the stairs to the dining room. Out of breath, we arrived just as Professor Bell was wiping his glass straw on a napkin.

"You again?" He shook his head at us and tucked the straw into his jacket pocket. "I thought you had left."

"We went upstairs for a minute," I explained. "But we came back." I cleared my throat and said loudly, "We came back to see you—Professor Bell."

"I am Mr. Thomas A. Watson," he said, standing to leave the room. "You are mistaken."

"We met the real Mr. Watson upstairs," I said. Then, I boldly blocked his way out of the room. "We need to talk to you, Professor. Just for a minute."

Professor Alexander Graham Bell didn't look like he wanted to talk to us. "I am so tired of electric speech, I will pay you to go away and never mention it again."

"How much?" Zack asked with a twinkle in his eye. It was hard to tell if he was serious or not, so I shoved him hard. Taking Alexander Graham Bell's money to leave was not an option.

I didn't know what to do. Then, I remembered the package. "We have a present for you from Mabel Hubbard." I held out the big, flat rectangle.

That did it! Alexander Graham Bell stepped back and sat down in a chair. "How do you know Mabel?" he asked.

"We went to her house looking for you," Jacob explained.

"How is she feeling today?" Alexander Graham Bell asked us.

Jacob took the package from me and handed it to Professor Bell. "She's feeling much better, but her father won't let her visit you today. She asked us to bring you this gift."

Alexander Graham Bell smiled. "It must be the painting. Mabel has been working on a portrait of me." He took the package from Jacob and tore off the paper.

It was a painting, all right. But not of Professor Bell.

It was a picture of a snowy owl.

Alexander Graham Bell held the picture high and looked at it long and hard.

Bo leaned over to me and whispered, "It's a painting of him. Get it?"

Mabel had said that Aleck worked with deaf students all day and invented all night. Owls are awake all night. She meant Alexander Graham Bell was like an owl. "I get it," I told Bo.

Alexander Graham Bell put down the painting. "Mabel likes it that I am going to quit," he told us. "After I finish the multiple telegraph, I will not be up all night anymore. Maybe someday she will paint a real portrait of me."

Bo took a deep breath and stepped forward. "The painting is funny, but the world needs you to be an owl a little longer."

"We need you to invent the telephone," I added.

"The electric speech apparatus," Jacob added, in case Professor Bell had forgotten the word "telephone."

"Come upstairs," Professor Bell said, and sighed. "I will show you exactly why I quit working on electric speech."

We walked back up the stairs with Alexander Graham Bell. My legs were feeling rubbery from going up and down the steps.

When we reached the landing, Alexander Graham Bell called to Mr. Watson to put the wire up between rooms 13 and 15.

Mr. Watson stepped into the hallway. "You want me to take it down. Then you want me to put it back up. You need to make up your mind."

"I *have* made up my mind. I have quit working on electric speech!" Professor Bell said firmly. "These pesky children are trying to convince me to keep trying." Mr. Watson handed Professor Bell a spool of wire. "I am going prove to them that the electric speech apparatus does not work. It will never work!"

We followed Professor Bell into room 15, his bedroom. He took one end of the wire and attached it to a small black cone. He gave the other end back to Mr. Watson. Mr. Watson went into the next room.

"At first, I wanted to invent something that would make the world easier for deaf people. My father invented an alphabet system that used symbols instead of letters to teach the deaf to communicate. So I thought if a deaf person could speak into a cone, a machine like a telegraph could write down his or her words on the other side. Then, I also got the idea that if two people could hear, maybe two voices could be transmitted electrically to each other." He sighed. "But neither idea works. Mabel's father thinks I should stick to the multiple telegraph instead of fiddle around with this foolishness."

"The telephone is going to be way more important than the multiple telegraph," I argued.

"Are you listening?" Alexander Graham Bell said, turning to face me. "It does not work! I do not know why. I cannot fix it. Electric speech will never happen."

"But electric speech *will* work," I insisted. "You just have to keep trying."

Alexander Graham Bell stared at me. I thought he was going to go crazy and start yelling at me. That's what my sister does when I keep badgering her about something. But, instead, he ruffled my hair and said, "You never give up, do you?"

"Mr. Watson," Alexander Graham Bell called down the hall to his assistant, "after we show these meddling children what a failure electric speech is, let us finish the multiple telegraph."

Alexander Graham Bell held the cone to his mouth. "Go next door," he told us.

We followed the wire down the hall to room 13. Mr. Watson had a similar black cone on his table.

We could hear Alexander Graham Bell talking. But not through the cone. He was shouting into the hallway, "Can you hear me?"

"Sure," Jacob answered. "But if we close the door, we won't."

"Change the tension on the reed," Professor Bell called down the hall. Mr. Watson reached over to the

bottom of his cone and tightened a screw.

There was a silent pause before Professor Bell shouted from the next room, "Did you hear me?"

"What did you say?" Mr. Watson shouted back. "I can't hear you!"

"I will attach the magnet," Professor Bell called out. There was another silent pause, followed by Professor Bell shouting, "How about that time?"

We all looked at Mr. Watson, hoping he could repeat whatever Professor Bell was saying in the other room. But Mr. Watson just shook his head at us.

"He can't hear you," Jacob called down the hall.

"See? It does not work!" Alexander Graham Bell shouted.

We went back to Alexander Graham Bell's bedroom.

"To make a voice travel over a wire, we need to make an electrical circuit," Professor Bell explained. "A circuit is a circle of electricity. Mr. Watson was working on the wires and electricity for the circuit. I was trying to figure out how the wires could carry voices, but I cannot do it. It cannot be done."

He removed the wire from the cone and left it on the table. Then, he leaned out the door and called to Mr. Watson, "Come here, please."

When Mr. Watson arrived, Professor Bell said, "For the last time, take down the wire." He was clearly frustrated. "There is no future for electric speech." Professor Bell threw up his hands and announced, "I quit!"

6

Fire

Alexander Graham Bell started throwing parts of his electric speech apparatus into a big wooden box.

I was worried. We needed a plan. And we needed one quickly. So we went out into the hallway to talk.

I suddenly had an idea. "I know what to do," I said excitedly.

"What?" Zack asked. He had an "I told you this was going be hard" look in his eyes.

"We have to show him there is a future for electric speech," I said. "And there is only one way to show him that!"

"A trip to the future?" Jacob asked, with one eyebrow raised. He was already thinking about where we should take Alexander Graham Bell. "We could take him to the mall," he suggested. "He could see people talking on cell phones while they shop."

"Bad idea," Bo said, scratching his chin again, deep in thought. "He's a tinkerer, remember? He might try to invent the cellular phone instead. We need him to invent phones with wires, not phones without wires."

"How about walking with him down Main Street?" I offered. "We could show him pay phones and phone books."

Zack threw out another idea: "How about to an office building? He could see video phones, fax machines, and speaker phones."

"Before we moved here, Mom and I lived with my *abuelo,* my grandfather, in New Mexico," Bo explained. "Maybe we should just take Professor Bell to my house and let him call Abuelo Rodriguez," he suggested. "He could see how we can talk on telephones to people who are far away."

We were ready to do everything we could to convince him, but the sound of a woman screaming outside interrupted our planning.

We all ran to the window.

A house down the street was on fire. We could see the flames shooting up through the roof.

We ran down the stairs and hurried outside. A woman ran up to us and asked us to help her.

"Did you call 9-1-1?" I asked her. She stared at me like I was crazy before running back down the street.

Alexander Graham Bell rushed out of the boardinghouse. "Ring the alarm!" he shouted to us. Then he hurried down the street to see what he could do to help.

"Ring the bell!" another man called out as he rushed past to help.

"Where's the fire alarm?" Jacob asked me.

I looked at Bo. He shrugged. Bo looked at Zack. Zack didn't know where the fire alarm was either. We started to run around in circles, looking for a way to call the firehouse.

Mr. Watson rushed by.

"Where's the fire alarm?" Jacob called out to him.

Mr. Watson pointed down the street to a black box hanging on a pole.

We ran down the street. Bo opened the box. When the door of the box swung open, little bells started tinkling. They made cute and happy sounds. Not the kind I'd expected from a fire alarm. I was positive that we had to do something else to call the fire department.

Inside the box was a telegraph machine similar to the one Mr. Caruthers had shown us in the library.

We gathered around the alarm box.

"How many dots and dashes in 'H-E-L-P'?" I asked Bo.

Bo looked at me blankly. Just because he'd read about telegrams didn't mean he knew how to send one.

We didn't know what to do. We had finally found the fire alarm box, but we didn't know how to send the telegraph. We couldn't ring the fire alarm.

"Hey, there's a little sign on the door," Zack said, looking over my shoulder. "It says, 'Pull the Hook.'"

I reached into the box and pulled down the small lever. It made the telegraph pieces come together, creating one huge, long dash.

And then we waited. And waited. And waited. Nothing happened.

Mr. Watson came over to us. "Did you pull the lever?" he asked.

"Yes," Jacob answered, "but nothing is happening."

"Oh yes, it is," Mr. Watson replied. "When there is a fire, we send a telegram from these street boxes. The telegram goes to a main office. The office tells the fire station about the fire. Then, the station sends the fire truck."

It seemed to take forever, but we finally saw the fire truck coming down the street.

"It's a steam fire engine like the one in the car museum Dad takes us to," Zack whispered to Jacob.

I looked down the street and saw six horses pulling the big, red fire engine.

The fire truck stopped right in front of Jacob, Zack, Bo, and me. Some firefighters pulled a long

hose out of the fire engine and attached it to a nearby fire hydrant.

Other firefighters threw logs into the fire truck's engine. The truck burned fuel, like wood sticks and logs, in a small steam engine. The steam engine provided power for a water pump. The water pump pumped water from the hydrant through the hose.

The firefighters held the hose high toward the fire. Water shot out of the hose in long bursts and fell on the flames.

Mr. Watson went to see if he could help.

It didn't take long for the firefighters to put the fire out. And when they did, Professor Bell and Mr. Watson came over to where we were standing.

"What a shame!" Professor Bell moaned. "The fire destroyed her house."

"At least it did not destroy the whole neighborhood," Mr. Watson said. He was covered with ash. He'd been helping the woman search for her dog in the rubble. He held a small puppy in his arms.

"Four years ago," Mr. Watson explained, "a fire burned down much of the city of Boston. It ate up more than 770 buildings, and it took three days before it stopped burning."

Mr. Watson saw the woman who owned the house sitting on the sidewalk. "I must go," he said. He went to give the woman her dog.

Professor Bell sighed and said, "If only we could call the fire engines faster than by telegram." He rubbed his tired eyes and added quietly, "We could save both lives and buildings."

"We can!" Zack said excitedly. "If you don't quit, we can!"

"Can what?" Professor Bell asked. He was confused.

"If you invent the telephone, we can get the fire engines to a fire faster," Jacob said. He grinned and got the computer out of his pocket.

Zack looked around to make sure no one was watching. "The coast is clear," he told his brother.

Jacob pushed a few buttons on the computer. Then he pulled the cartridge out of the back slot.

A green, glowing hole appeared in the street near the black telegraph box. Thick smoke covered the ground.

"What is that?" Alexander Graham Bell asked, curiously inspecting the big hole. As he moved closer to the hole, I saw a mischievous spark in the twins' eyes.

"What are you guys doing?" I asked them.

Jacob and Zack answered at exactly the same time: "We are talking Alexander Graham Bell to meet our dad!"

Zack pushed Alexander Graham Bell into the hole.

Bo, Jacob, and I held hands.

On the count of three, we jumped.

And on the count of four, we landed, because time travel is really fast.

7

The Future

Jacob and Zack's dad was a firefighter. I knew that because I lived next door to them. Sometimes their dad worked all night. He'd be coming home to go to sleep when Jacob and Zack were leaving for school.

Today, Firefighter Osborn was working at the firehouse. We landed at the front door of the station.

"What is the meaning of this?" Professor Bell demanded to know. "Where are we?"

"Would you believe us if we told you we have traveled to the future?" Jacob asked.

"No!" Professor Bell said loudly. "I would not believe you."

"Even if it was the truth?" Bo questioned.

"I am a scientist," Professor Bell proclaimed. "Can you prove to me that we are in your time and not in mine?"

"Easy," I said, looking around for something to show him. "Come with me." We walked down the front path and around the corner.

A big, red fire truck was parked in the garage. "See?" I said. "Cars and trucks weren't invented in eighteen seventy-six."

"I see what you mean," Professor Bell said as he climbed up into the driver's seat. "I am beginning to believe you. Is this a fire engine from your time?"

"It's a little different from the ones you have in eighteen seventy-six," Jacob said. "This one has an engine with a battery. Instead of steam."

"A battery," Professor Bell repeated. "That is interesting."

"You'd better get him out of there," Bo said to me. "He's a tinkerer, remember. If we don't pay attention, he might just decide to invent the first car, or truck, or—"

"Battery," Professor Bell repeated again. He hopped

down from the fire truck. "Can I see the battery?"

"No!" we all said at once.

"I'm sorry, Professor Bell," I explained. "We're supposed to convince you to get back to work on the telephone. We can't let you invent something else instead."

"But—," Professor Bell countered.

"Sorry," I interrupted.

"Excuse me," a loud voice said from behind us. "You are not allowed in the fire truck." I turned around to see Jacob and Zack's dad coming out of the firehouse and into the garage.

"Hi," Firefighter Osborn said when he saw Jacob, Zack, Bo, and me. "I thought you kids had History Club today after school." He looked at Jacob and Zack. "I'd better call Mom and tell her you're here."

"Wait, Dad," Jacob said quickly. "This is today's History Club activity." We liked to call our time-travel adventures "History Club." It was pretty much true: We met after school and we were trying to save history. "We'll be back at school in time for Mom to pick us up," he quickly added.

Zack checked the clock on the wall and mumbled, "Hopefully," under his breath.

"Hello, Firefighter Osborn," I said. "This is our special History Club teacher, Professor Bell." The two men shook hands. "Professor Bell was showing us how telegraphs were used to call fire trucks in eighteen seventy-six," I explained. "We wanted to find out if today's telephone system was faster."

"It's much faster," Firefighter Osborn said. "All over America, there are more than 500,000 emergency calls to 9-1-1 every day. That's about 190 million a year. Telegraphs took too long to send, and it was difficult to figure out exactly where the fire was. Calling 9-1-1 on the telephone saves thousands of lives each day."

"Is that so?" Professor Bell seemed interested.

Firefighter Osborn apologized that he had to rush off and check a fire hose. "I'll be right back."

While he was gone, I whispered to Professor Bell, "In our time, pretty much everyone has a telephone. There are telephones in our houses that work on wires. And there are cellular phones that we can carry around that don't have any wires at all."

"And you can report an emergency from both kinds of telephones?" he asked me.

"Sure," I said. "Are you convinced now?"

"We only have fifty-two minutes to get him back to finish the invention," Jacob said softly.

I tugged at Alexander Graham Bell's arm. I hoped we'd told him enough about telephones to convince him to not quit inventing. It was time for him to get back to his boardinghouse. There was a good spot behind the firehouse to open the green hole.

"I do not understand your hurry," Professor Bell said. "I would like to explore this city of the future. I have all the time in the world." He grinned at us. "I quit inventing electric speech, remember?"

"We remember," I said, and sighed. "But we still hope you'll change your mind."

Professor Bell was being difficult. He wasn't going to be convinced easily.

Firefighter Osborn came back and invited us inside the firehouse. He showed us the kitchen. He showed us the bunkrooms, where firefighters rest when they aren't working.

And he showed us a small room where the telephones were kept.

It was a little office. There was a desk with a computer and two telephones. One was attached to the wall. Another was sitting on the desk by the computer.

Suddenly, the phone on the wall rang.

Firefighter Osborn answered, talked for a minute, and hung up. "Firefighter Wong is calling from her house. She thinks she left her wallet in the bunkroom. I'm going to check. I think I saw it upstairs. I'll be right back." He left us alone in the office.

After Firefighter Osborn left the room, Professor Bell moved closer to the telephone on the desk. He poked at it with his finger. Then he picked up the receiver. "Aha!" he exclaimed. "It *is* my electric speech apparatus! Wires and all!"

"Telephone," I corrected, hoping that this would be the moment when he'd change his mind and want to go back to inventing.

"Telephone," he repeated. He was pretty calm for a man who was seeing what his invention would look like more than one hundred years later.

"Look!" Jacob said. "It works just like the one you and Mr. Watson are building." He held out the receiver to show him. "You talk in here," he said, pointing to the bottom of the receiver. "And you listen from here." He showed Professor Bell the top part of the phone.

Professor Bell put his ear to the receiver and jumped back suddenly. "What do I hear?" he asked. He looked really confused.

"A dial tone," Bo answered. And because Bo had read more than any of us, he knew how to explain. "The telephone works on an electrical circuit."

We knew that the reason Professor Bell quit inventing the telephone was because he couldn't get the circuit to work correctly. But we also knew that if we could get him back to 1876 and convince him to keep trying, he'd figure it out.

Bo continued: "Our telephones make a circuit with a central office. The office gives each person a different telephone number, which is his or her personal circuit. When you lift the receiver, you hear the dial tone, which means your circuit is ready for you to make a phone call."

"The circuit is always ready?" Professor Bell asked.

"Yes," Bo answered.

Professor Bell bit his lip and mumbled, "Battery."

I had no idea what he was talking about.

Professor Bell was looking at the telephone pad on the wall. "These are the numbers?" He pressed a few buttons.

"Careful," Zack said. "If you press the numbers, you'll call someone. The central office automatically connects you with the number you dialed and completes the call."

"We usually only call people if we know their phone number," Jacob added. "And we only call 9-1-1 if there is an emergency."

Professor Bell hung up the phone. Then he picked it up again.

Professor Bell kept picking up the receiver, listening to the dial tone, shaking his head, and then hanging up again. I could see that he was thinking.

I hoped that he was ready to get back to inventing.

If we left now, he'd still have enough time to figure out how to make electric speech work.

Brring. The loud ringing of the fire alarm echoed through the firehouse.

We heard footsteps as the firefighters rushed to get dressed and onto the fire truck. Some firefighters slid down the fire pole. Others were putting on their boots, coveralls, and hats. Everyone was getting ready to go out and fight a fire.

Firefighter Osborn stuck his head in the office. "You kids stay here with Professor Bell. Don't follow me to the fire. It could be dangerous. I'll be back as soon as I can." He rushed off to get his gear.

When another firefighter hurried into the office to check the computer, we moved out into the hall. The firehouse was suddenly crowded with firefighters rushing past us, heading toward the garage. We pressed back against a wall, trying to stay out of their way.

We had shown Professor Bell everything we could. We couldn't show him how fast the fire trucks could get to an emergency. He'd have to trust us that his invention helped save many lives every day.

"Professor Bell?" I asked, turning my head to tell the inventor that it was time to go home. But he wasn't there! I looked around. He wasn't standing with us in the hall. "Where'd he go? I swear he was just here a second ago."

"I tried to stop him," Zack said. He pointed out the door of the garage.

We rushed out to the driveway. The fire truck was turning the street corner.

I squinted to see where Zack was pointing and couldn't believe my eyes.

Professor Bell was waving at us from the back of the fire truck!

8

9-1-1

"What happened?" I asked Bo.

"He can run really fast," Bo answered.

"So can Zack," I replied. "Zack's the fastest runner in the whole third grade."

"I think Alexander Graham Bell might be faster," Jacob said. "Professor Bell ran and jumped onto the truck while it was leaving. Zack ran after him and tried to block his way, but Professor Bell was too quick."

"We're in trouble," Zack groaned. "The fire truck could be going anywhere in the city."

"That's not exactly true," Jacob said. "This station is only for a small part of the city. Only the firehouse closest to the fire sends trucks."

"Unless there is a big emergency," Bo said. "Then, many firehouses send their trucks." It really didn't matter how far away the fire truck went. It was just plain bad that it had left. And that Professor Bell had gone with it.

We were in big trouble.

"We could wait until they get back," I suggested. It wasn't a great plan, but it was the only idea I had.

"That would take too much time," Jacob said, checking his watch. "We have only forty-three minutes to get Professor Bell back to eighteen seventy-six."

"And to get him to invent the telephone," Bo added.

It seemed like things couldn't be any worse, but Jacob was smiling. "I can solve one of our problems," he said, grinning so wide, all his teeth showed.

"How?" I asked.

Jacob led us all back into the firehouse. Next to the telephone was a computer

"Can you find the fire truck?" Bo asked Jacob.

"Sure," Jacob said as he sat down at the desk. "This computer keeps track of where 9-1-1 calls come from," he explained while he pushed a few letters on the keyboard. Numbers flashed across the screen. "When a person calls 9-1-1, an emergency operator answers the phone. The operator asks some important questions to decide what kind of help the person needs."

Jacob was still sitting at the computer pressing buttons. He continued: "In some cities, they have new computers that can figure out addresses. No one needs to tell the operators where to send help. The computer can figure it out on its own."

"And the best part is," Zack added, "Dad told me that if you call 9-1-1, it usually takes less than a minute for help to be on the way."

"Boy, if only we could have called 9-1-1 in eighteen seventy-six," I said, shaking my head, "maybe that woman's house wouldn't have burned down. Telegrams sure took a lot longer than telephones."

"Too long," Zack agreed.

Bo leaned over Jacob's shoulder and read the information. "A woman called 9-1-1 from 324 High Street. There is a fire in her kitchen."

"Oh, no!" My heart started beating so fast, I thought it might explode. "I live at 322 High Street! Right next door!"

"We live at 320 High Street!" Jacob and Zack shouted at the same time.

"It's our neighbor Mrs. Kapalsky!" I said. "She might need help because she can't hear the fire engine's siren. She's deaf!"

"Just like Mabel," Bo said.

"Yes," I said quickly.

"We'd better run!" Zack was out the door before the rest of us were ready to go.

"Jacob, we need to hurry. Tie your shoe!" I said, and poked him in the arm.

Jacob refused and took off running after Zack.

Bo and I rushed out of the firehouse. We went running down the street and around the corner. We scooted past my house and got to Mrs. Kapalsky's house just as the firefighters were packing up the truck to return to the fire station.

"What happened?" I asked Zack. He'd gotten to Mrs. Kapalsky's house a little before me.

"She put too much oil in a pan. It bubbled and made a small fire in her kitchen. Dad was able to put it out quickly," Zack answered. Jacob and Bo came to stand beside us.

"Mrs. Kapalsky is fine," Bo said. "Because they got here so fast, the firefighters saved her house."

I was just about to ask if any of the boys had seen Mrs. Kapalsky, when I saw her standing on the front lawn talking to Professor Bell and Firefighter Osborn. They were standing in a small circle. They had their heads close together.

Professor Bell was talking with his hands. He was speaking in sign language to Mrs. Kapalsky. Mrs. Kapalsky handed a white square box to Professor Bell and gave him a kiss on the cheek. She gave Firefighter Osborn a hug.

I discovered I could read lips, too, when I saw her say "thank you" to the two men.

She saw us standing in the driveway. She waved and went back inside her house.

Firefighter Osborn went over to talk to another firefighter. Professor Bell came over to us. He was very excited. "The fire is out. Everyone is safe. And I have two important things to show you."

I'd never seen Professor Bell so happy. I liked him best when he wasn't quitting, tricking us, or running away.

Professor Bell showed us the white box he was holding. "This is Mrs. Kapalsky's Teletype machine," he explained. "Mrs. Kapalsky uses this machine like a telephone. She can call her friends. She just types in her message instead of speaking. And her friends write back." He pressed a few numbers on the keypad. "A teletypewriter is a combination of the electric speech apparatus and a multiple telegraph machine. The typing travels through the voice wires used for telephone circuits."

"Did she call 9-1-1 by Teletype?" Zack asked.

"Exactly," Professor Bell said, and smiled at Zack.

Now it made sense how the computer at the fire station had known Mrs. K's address. She'd called 9-1-1 on her own. Mrs. K didn't need to be able to hear to call for help.

I suddenly understood why Mr. C hadn't called on

me in class. He'd known I was too curious to let it slide. Mr. C had wanted me to ask him why he'd ignored me, so that he could give me a useful time-travel clue.

When he'd answered, "I didn't mean to turn a deaf ear," he was hinting that to understand Alexander Graham Bell, we had to understand the world of the deaf. Alexander Graham Bell didn't set out to invent the telephone so that my friends and I could make plans to go to the mall; he wanted to create something that would make the world a better place for deaf people.

And he did it! Even though she couldn't hear, the Teletype machine saved Mrs. Kapalsky's house. And her life.

Mrs. Kapalsky was able to call 9-1-1 by Teletype!

A firefighter was standing near us. Professor Bell walked over to him and handed him the Teletype machine. "This is Mrs. Kapalsky's," he told the firefighter. "She said I could borrow it to show my friends. Would you please give it back to her for me?"

The firefighter agreed, took the machine, and headed into the house.

The Teletype machine was the first important thing Alexander Graham Bell wanted us to see. "What's the second thing you wanted to show us?" I asked.

"Come with me," he said.

We followed Professor Bell over to the front of a fire truck. "After the fire was out, I asked Firefighter Osborn to show me the truck's engine and battery." He climbed up into the driver's seat.

We couldn't all fit in the truck's cab, so we waited for him to explain.

"I have had a breakthrough. It is the battery!" he called as he took the last step up into the truck. "The fire truck has a battery tucked under the driver's seat," Professor Bell shouted from high up in the truck. He ducked down under the front seat. We couldn't see him anymore.

Zack leaned toward me and grunted. "I told you it was going to be hard to get him to go back to phones. Now we've really made a mess. He's going to try to invent a car or truck instead of the telephone."

"No!" Professor Bell shouted from the cab of the truck. "I am going back to eighteen seventy-six. I am going to invent the telephone. I figured out why the electric speech apparatus does not work!"

Zack looked surprised. "Well," he said with a shrug, "for the first time in history, I was wrong." We all started to laugh. "Professor Bell is going back to inventing the telephone. You know what this means, don't you?"

We didn't.

"It's the sad end of the multiple telegraph," Zack said, pretending to cry. We all laughed again. Zack had been right. It had been extra hard to convince Professor Bell to try to invent the phone after he quit. But now he was willing to try again. I crossed my fingers that whatever he saw in the truck would help.

"The secret to the telephone is battery acid," Professor Bell cheered. He popped out of the truck and dropped to the ground.

"When can I go home?" Professor Bell asked us. He was talking quickly. He couldn't wait to get back to Mr. Watson and the boardinghouse. "I am ready to try again! I will try until I get it right!" Professor Bell put his hand on Jacob's head and messed up his hair. "You kids showed me how my invention will help people who are deaf *and* people who can hear." Professor Bell was very happy.

Jacob pulled the computer out of his pocket. He was all set to put in the cartridge when Firefighter Osborn called, "Boys!" from across the yard. Jacob quickly stashed the computer back in his pocket.

Firefighter Osborn came over to us. His eyes were dark. I was scared we were in big trouble. We had followed him to the fire when he'd told us not to.

"You shouldn't be here," he said. "I understand that you were worried about Mrs. Kapalsky, but I told you to wait at the firehouse." He wasn't smiling.

"I was my fault," Alexander Graham Bell told Firefighter Osborn. "I rode on the fire truck. The children were worried that they would not find me again."

It was nice of Professor Bell to stick up for us. But it didn't work.

"The kids know better than to come around a fire," Firefighter Osborn told Professor Bell. "They should have waited at the firehouse for you to return." Then he put his big hands on his sons' heads. "Jacob and Zack are grounded for a week." He looked at me. "I'll call your parents later tonight." Then he turned to Bo. "And I'll call your mom tonight too."

Firefighter Osborn said good-bye to Professor Bell and walked away. He jumped on the fire truck for the trip back to the firehouse. "Don't forget to be back at school by five o'clock. Mom will be waiting."

I was bummed. I knew I'd be grounded too.

"What does 'grounded' mean?" Alexander Graham Bell asked me.

"No television for a whole week," I moaned.

"Since I do not know what a television is," Professor Bell said, "it does not sound like a terrible punishment to me."

When he put it that way, it didn't sound so bad to

me, either. Maybe I'd check out a book on Alexander Graham Bell from the school library and catch up on my reading.

Bo, the twins, and I walked with Professor Bell to a quiet place in Mrs. Kapalsky's yard.

"Can I take us home?" Professor Bell held out his hand.

Jacob gave him the computer.

"I would like to invent a time-travel machine," Professor Bell said as he slipped in the cartridge. Green glowing smoke filled the street. A big hole opened near Mrs. Kapalsky's flower pot. "But first I have to invent the electric speech apparatus." Professor Bell handed Jacob the computer.

"Can you finish the invention in twenty-six minutes?" Jacob asked, looking down into the deep hole.

"I hope so," Professor Bell said, taking my hand in his. "But we will never know unless I try."

We all linked hands, forming a circle. I counted to three. And we jumped.

9

Tinkering

We dashed up the boardinghouse stairs.

"Hang the wire!" Professor Bell shouted to Mr. Watson.

Professor Bell opened his bedroom door and rushed inside. He didn't care that he had twenty-six minutes to make history. He thought he knew how to make electric speech work and he was excited to try his new idea.

Mr. Watson walked slowly into the room. "You quit, remember?"

"The children convinced me to not quit. We have to keep trying until we get this apparatus to transmit sound!" Professor Bell picked up the wooden box he'd put the apparatus pieces into and dumped the contents onto the floor.

As he gathered the pieces he needed, Professor Bell said, "With the telephone, it is possible to connect every man's house, office, or factory with a central station, so as to give him direct communication with his neighbors."

Bo leaned over and whispered to me, "You just heard history. Alexander Graham Bell wrote those exact words in a letter in eighteen seventy-eight."

"How do you know?" I asked.

"I like to read, remember?" Bo replied, smiling.

Jacob turned to Professor Bell and asked, "What can we do to help you?"

Alexander Graham Bell was making a huge mess. He was throwing wires and magnets, needles and screws all over the floor. "Abigail," he said to me. "You and Bo help Mr. Watson rehang the wire."

"Twins," he said, looking at Jacob and Zack, "I need some battery acid."

"I'm not sure where to get some," Zack said truthfully.

"Go with Mr. Watson next door. He'll give you some." Professor Bell took a handful of supplies off the floor and put them on his desk. "Put some in a jar. Mix in a little water, and then bring the liquid back here." Suddenly, Alexander Graham Bell became very quiet.

He was thinking hard. We didn't want to interrupt. So we got to work.

When the wire was hung, Zack carried the jar of battery acid back to Professor Bell.

"The fire truck's battery gave me the idea. Battery acid is a very strong conductor. I think it might be exactly what we need to make the circuit work. I think if I use a metal needle"—he worked as he talked—"and put the needle in a mixture of water and battery acid—" Professor Bell suddenly stopped talking again.

He got up from the desk. He attached a wire between the battery and the needle. He used a second wire to connect the battery to the metal cone. Then he used screws to attach the whole apparatus to Mr. Watson's wire.

Alexander Graham Bell poured the water and battery acid mixture into the cone.

"See? It's a complete circuit." Bo showed me. "The wires go in a circle from the battery to the cone to the needle, over to Mr. Watson's room, then back around."

While Professor Bell was thinking about what else he needed to do, we all ran next door to see what Mr. Watson was up to.

He had taken the wire that connected the two rooms and attached it to an electromagnetic receiver and a metal plate. When Professor Bell spoke, the metal plate was supposed to vibrate and change the electricity into words.

Mr. Watson put the receiver up to his ear.

We all stood silently, waiting for the first telephone call.

Nothing happened.

I could hear Professor Bell talking, but it was from the hallway—not from the electric speech apparatus.

"Bummer," Zack said.

"He has only nine minutes left," Jacob said after checking his watch.

I was super nervous. Could he figure it out in time?

Mr. Watson tightened the screws on his receiver. He put the cone back up to his ear.

Nothing.

We hurried back next door to see what Professor Bell was doing.

He was talking softly down into the cone. The needle was bobbing up and down at the bottom of the liquid. But it still wasn't working.

His face was red. He was frustrated. I was worried he'd quit again.

We had to do something. Time was running out, and he hadn't invented the telephone yet! "Jacob," I said quickly. "You know how to make things work. Go help him."

"I guess I could try," Jacob agreed. But just as Jacob stepped closer to Alexander Graham Bell, the professor stood up. He turned to us, holding the cone filled with battery acid, and said, "Maybe I was wrong." He began to move toward Jacob, but his foot got tangled up and he tripped.

Professor Bell tried to catch his balance. But it was too late. He crashed into the desk and tipped the cone over. Battery acid spilled all over Professor Bell's legs.

We all turned and looked at Alexander Graham Bell's wet pants. And his wet shoes.

He bent over his desk and picked up the fallen cone. There was a little bit of battery acid left in the bottom, barely enough liquid to cover the end of the needle. Alexander Graham Bell put the cone down on the desk.

He was going to need some serious help cleaning up the mess.

"Mr. Watson, come here, I want to see you!" Alexander Graham Bell said firmly.

And to our surprise, a happy shout came from next door. "We did it!" Mr. Watson screamed down the hall. "It works!" He came running into the room. "Professor Bell, I heard every word you said—distinctly!" Mr. Watson had heard Professor

Bell's call for help through the receiver he held to his ear.

Alexander Graham Bell and Mr. Watson were very happy. Jacob and Zack showed them how to do high fives. And some low fives too.

"Less liquid in the cone! That was the answer," Professor Bell cheered. He turned to look at Jacob. "Thank you, Jacob."

"I'm glad I could help," Jacob said, reaching out to shake Professor Bell's hand. "Wait a minute," Jacob suddenly said, pulling back his hand. "Why are you thanking me?"

"I tripped on your shoelace, me boy," Alexander Graham Bell said with a laugh. "It was a good thing you didn't tie it."

"But I did!" Jacob shouted. "I tied it just before we did the T.T. to come back here."

"T.T.?" Alexander Graham Bell asked with a curious look on his face.

"Time travel," Zack translated. We all looked down. Jacob's shoelace was wrapped in a neat bow.

"But if Jacob didn't make Professor Bell fall, what happened?" I wondered aloud.

Alexander Graham Bell choked on a short spurt of laughter. He gave Jacob a hearty pat on the back and began to chuckle even harder. "You are correct," he said, and pointed down. "It was me own silly lace that did the trick!"

I looked at his shoe and then up at Alexander Graham Bell. "You fell over your own untied shoelace!" I exclaimed in surprise. I was about to say something else about shoelaces, when suddenly, a loud beeping sound came from Jacob's pocket.

The computer was warning us that we had only thirty seconds left. It was time for us to go.

"Good luck with the electric speech apparatus," I quickly said instead.

"You mean the 'telephone,'" Professor Bell said, and winked.

We said good-bye. Then, Jacob held up the computer and pulled out the cartridge. The green hole opened near Professor Bell's desk.

"What is that?" Mr. Watson asked. He stepped close to the hole.

Alexander Graham Bell pulled him back by the arm. "Do not go too close," he said to Mr. Watson, grinning. "I will explain it to you later. Right now, we have to get back to our electric speech apparatus. We have much work to do before people can call 9-1-1." Professor Bell winked at us.

Zack and Bo jumped first.

Jacob and I were ready to jump when we heard Professor Bell call after us, "Jacob, your shoe is untied again. You should tie it."

"I'll tie mine if you tie yours," Jacob answered him with a smile.

Just as our feet hit the hole, I heard Professor Bell whoop with laughter.

10

Home Again

"Two hours, zero seconds," Jacob announced. We were back at school. We landed outside near the playground.

"We did it!" Bo did a little happy dance.

"We fixed history!" I joined Bo in the dance.

Zack gave high fives to everyone. "I knew we could do it!"

"You're kidding, right?" Jacob said to Zack.

"I said it wasn't going to be easy," Zack said. "I never said it was impossible."

"Well, if Professor Bell can go back to the telephone, maybe someday you'll go back to Theater Club or Science Club."

"Maybe," Zack answered, rubbing his chin like Bo always did. "You never know."

"Come on. Let's go tell Mr. Caruthers what happened," I suggested.

We found Mr. Caruthers back in the library.

"We're back," Jacob told him.

Mr. Caruthers was sitting on the couch looking at his own copy of the book *Famous People in American History.*

He held up the book and smiled. "Shall we see how you did?"

"We—," Bo began.

Mr. Caruthers put a finger over his lips. "Shh. Don't tell me." He handed me the book. "If history has changed, Alexander Graham Bell's telephone won't be in this book anymore."

I read the chapter title out loud: "'Alexander Graham Bell and His Many Inventions.'"

Mr. Caruthers told me to turn to page 56.

I flipped through the pages. There it was. A picture of the electric speech apparatus.

I pointed at the picture. There was the cone with

the battery acid. And the screws where Alexander Graham Bell attached the wire that we had hung with Mr. Watson.

Under the photo was a painting of the boarding-house room. Mr. Watson and Professor Bell were standing in the room. The electric speech apparatus was on the desk. And on the wall was the snowy owl portrait Mabel had made. I turned the book to show the boys.

"Good job," Mr. Caruthers said. "Did you know that there was another man trying to invent the telephone at the same time as Alexander Graham Bell?"

Bo answered softly. We all leaned in to hear him. "Do you mean Elisha Gray?"

"Yes," Mr. Caruthers said. "Elisha Gray was very close to inventing a telephone when Alexander Graham Bell finished his. Some people still think that Alexander Graham Bell stole the idea for using battery acid in the cone from Elisha Gray."

"Why do they think that?" I asked.

"Well," Mr. Caruthers explained, "in all the papers that Alexander Graham Bell wrote about inventing the telephone, he never mentioned using a liquid. In fact, he never tried using battery acid until March 10, 1876."

Bo knew the rest. "I read that Elisha Gray's notes all mentioned using a liquid, like battery acid, to conduct the electricity."

"Right," Mr. Caruthers told Bo.

I thought about that. Could Alexander Graham Bell have stolen the idea for battery acid from Elisha Gray? No way. I knew he got the idea from looking inside Firefighter Osborn's fire truck!

"The other thing," Mr. Caruthers added, "is that no one knows for sure if the story of the first telephone call is true or not."

"The story?" Zack asked. "What story?"

Mr. Caruthers look at Zack strangely before explaining. "The myth is that Professor Bell spilled battery acid on his pants and called for Mr. Watson's help. But no one knows if it's true."

I thought about that one too.

It was funny. You can be there. You can see history happen. You can be part of a historic event. But more than 127 years later, no one is sure what really happened.

They are just glad that it did.

And like everyone else, we were glad Professor Alexander Graham Bell hadn't quit.

A honking horn made us look out the library window.

"Gotta go," Jacob said. "Mom's here."

"Is baby Gabe with her?" I loved Zack and Jacob's baby brother. Gabe was almost two years old, but everyone still calls him "baby Gabe." He was really cute.

"I think she brought him. She usually does," Zack said. "Do you and Bo want a ride home?"

Bo had his bike at school, so he didn't need a ride.

"No thanks," I said. "I'll walk." I wanted some more time alone to think about Alexander Graham Bell and how his invention changed the world.

Mr. C pulled a little notebook out of his pocket. I had seen that notebook before. It was his list of famous Americans throughout history. We didn't know why, but for some strange reason, all the people on Mr. C's list were quitting. He flipped through a few pages, running his finger down the list of names.

Suddenly his finger stopped, and he pressed his lips together. "Hmm," he hummed with a long breath. "It looks like I'll need you kids again next Monday. Let's meet in the classroom after school." Mr. Caruthers waved to us as we left the library.

I couldn't stop smiling the whole way home.

Next Monday we would have another adventure. We would go back in history to convince someone else not to quit and give up a dream.

I could hardly wait.

Painting by W. A. Rogers. Picture copyright © National Geographic Society.

On February 7, 1918, Professor Alexander Graham Bell wrote:

"Leave the beaten track occasionally and dive into the woods. Every time you do so you will be certain to find something that you have never seen before. Follow it up, explore all around it, and before you know it, you will have something worth thinking about to occupy your mind. All really big discoveries are the results of thought."

This painting is by W. A. Rogers. It shows one of the rooms used by Alexander Graham Bell at 5 Exeter Place, Boston, Massachusetts. In the painting, Professor Bell is showing his electric speech apparatus to his assistant, Thomas A. Watson. Mr. Watson is the man standing on the left.

Do you see the picture of the snowy owl on the wall? Mabel Hubbard made this painting as a joke because Professor Bell would stay up all night working.

A Letter to Our Readers

Hi! We hope you enjoyed *Blast to the Past: Bell's Breakthrough.*

Bell's Breakthrough is a mixture of fiction and history. The time-travel part is fiction. No one we know has really time-traveled—at least not yet. But the story of Alexander Graham Bell and the invention of the telephone is true . . . well, mostly true.

Because his mother was deaf, Alexander Graham Bell was interested in sound and why some people heard sounds while others could not. He spent his life teaching deaf students and their teachers. His wife, Mable Hubbard, was also deaf.

When Alexander Graham Bell first had the idea for the telephone, he knew a lot about ears and sound vibrations, but he didn't know anything about electronics. Or how to pay for his inventions. Luckily, Alexander Graham Bell had friends to help him.

Thomas A. Watson was the machinist who helped Alexander Graham Bell make an electric circuit.

Mable's father, Gardiner Greene Hubbard, raised money for some of Alexander Graham Bell's inventions. And Mable helped "Aleck" by supporting him and encouraging his dreams. She painted the famous portrait of Alexander Graham Bell as a snowy owl.

As far as we know, Alexander Graham Bell never really quit. Even though he was a tinkerer and worked on a lot of different inventions, he spent a lot of time and energy inventing the telephone. He thought it would help make the lives of deaf people easier. But instead, the telephone has made life better for everyone!

It is true that a big fire destroyed much of Boston three years before Alexander Graham Bell invented the telephone. We think he would have liked learning about the 9-1-1 telephone system and how his invention saves lives.

The last bit of the story, where Alexander Graham Bell spilled battery acid on his legs and Thomas Watson heard him calling, well, no one knows for sure if that is a true story or a myth. It is up to you to decide. And while you are deciding things, no one will ever know if Alexander Graham Bell got the idea for using battery acid from Elisha Gray or not. Until someone really does invent a time-travel machine, there are a lot of questions about Alexander Graham Bell and the invention of the telephone that remain unanswered.

If you want to learn more about the series or want to contact us, you can visit our Web site at www.BlastToThePastBooks.com.

Enjoy!
Stacia and Rhody

Here's a sneak peek at the
fourth book in the

series:

King's Courage,
all about Martin Luther King Jr.

Coming Spring 2006!

Baby Gabe slipped the cartridge into the back of the machine. A time-travel hole opened in the classroom floor. Green smoke oozed out and floated around the room. Gabe was holding the computer, standing at the edge of the hole. Giggling.

I reached out quickly, snagging the back of his little blue pants. Unfortunately, the waistband was elastic. It stretched. And stretched. And stretched.

Bo grabbed me around the waist to steady me. Jacob put his arms around Bo. Zack held on to Jacob.

It was no use. With a quick turn of his head, Gabe sunk his teeth into my skin and bit me on the hand. "Ouch!" I shouted, opening my palm in pain.

Just like that … Baby Gabe toppled over and disappeared.

"We've got to go get Gabe!" I shouted to the boys, motioning to Zack to grab the diaper bag.

It was my turn to break the sound barrier as I leapt quickly, following Gabe down into the hole.

As I fell through time, I distinctly heard Jacob call out, "That mini-monster better not have broken Mr. C's computer!"

• • •

"Look!" I shouted suddenly. "Over there!" I pointed into the crowd.

Somehow, Martin Luther King Jr. had gotten by us. We never even saw him leave the church. He was walking quickly, disappearing into the mob.

I panicked. Dr. King was getting farther and farther away. I wanted to run after him, but we'd made a promise to Zack. We were going to find his brother, Gabe, first. As soon as we found Baby Gabe, we'd have to figure out how to catch up with Dr. King.

"Hey! Check it out!" Jacob was jumping up and down, pointing his finger like crazy.

Just behind Dr. King, an older black man had a small white boy riding on his shoulders. With my eagle eyes I could tell that the boy was wearing blue pants and a bright red shirt. Something in his hands glinted in the sunlight. It was Mr. C's computer.

We'd found him!

Baby Gabe was being carried off toward the Edmund Pettus Bridge—the start of the five-day march for voter rights for African Americans!